For Elise Tsenti
with love from J.W.

To Vanessa
T.R.

First published in Great Britain in 2008 by Andersen Press Ltd., 20 Vauxhall Bridge Road, London SW1V 2SA.
Published in Australia by Random House Australia Pty., Level 3, 100 Pacific Highway, North Sydney, NSW 2060.
Text copyright © Jeanne Willis, 2008. Illustrations copyright © Tony Ross, 2008.
The rights of Jeanne Willis and Tony Ross to be identified as the author and illustrator of this
work have been asserted by them in accordance with the Copyright, Designs and Patents Act, 1988.
All rights reserved. Colour separated in Switzerland by Photolitho AG, Zürich.
Printed and bound in Singapore.

10   9   8   7   6   5   4   3   2   1

British Library Cataloguing in Publication Data available.

ISBN 978 1 84270 659 6

This book has been printed on acid-free paper

Mammoth Pie

Jeanne Willis / Tony Ross

Andersen Press • London

On top of a mountain there lived a fat mammoth.
Down in the valley there lived a thin caveman.
The caveman was hungry. Very, very hungry.
He saw the mammoth and licked his lips.

He was fed up with eating seeds.
He was fed up with eating weeds.
"*Meat* is what a caveman needs!" said Og.
"I'll catch the mammoth and put him in a pie!"

The mammoth thought, "I'd like to see him try!
He's very thin and there's only one of him.
I'm very fat. I could squash him flat.
He has no spear to hit me.

He has no trap to trip me,
No cart to carry me, no pot to hold me.
He has no fire to cook me.
He'll never catch me and put me in a pie!"

Og couldn't catch the mammoth on his own.
So he went to ask his friends for help.
He went to see his old friend Ug.
He said to Ug, "Make me a spear!"

"Why? What will I get in return?" said Ug.
"A bite of Mammoth Pie!" said Og.
"Meat is what I need!" said Ug.
So he agreed to make the spear.

Og had a spear to hit the mammoth.
But he needed a trap to trip it.
He went to see his old friend Gog.
He said to Gog, "Dig me a trap!"

"Why? What will I get in return?" said Gog.
"A bite of Mammoth Pie!" said Og.
"Meat is what I need!" said Gog.
So he agreed to dig a trap.

Og had a trap to trip the mammoth.
But he needed a cart to carry it.
He went to see his old friend Bog.
He said to Bog, "Make me a cart!"

"Why? What will I get in return?" said Bog.
"A bite of Mammoth Pie!" said Og.
"Meat is what I need!" said Bog.
So he agreed to make a cart.

Og had a spear and a trap and a cart.
But he needed a pot to hold the mammoth.
He went to see his old friend Nog.
He said to Nog, "Make me a pot!"

"Why? What will I get in return?" said Nog.
"A bite of Mammoth Pie!" said Og.
"Meat is what I need!" said Nog.
So he agreed to make a pot.

Og had a spear, a trap, a cart and a pot.
But he needed a fire to cook the mammoth.
He went to see his old friend Mog.
He said to Mog, "Make me a fire!"

"Why? What will I get in return?" said Mog.
"A bite of Mammoth Pie!" said Og.
"Meat is what I need!" said Mog.
So he agreed to make a fire.

"Ready?" said Og. So off they jogged,
Ug and Gog, Bog, Nog and Mog.
As they jogged, they sang a song.
They sang it as they jogged along.

"We're fed up with eating weeds!
No more weeds! No more seeds!
Meat is what a caveman needs!
Meat is what a caveman needs!"

The mammoth saw the cavemen coming.
Up the mountainside they came.
Og had the spear. Gog set the trap.
Ug and Bog came with the cart.

Nog had the great big cooking pot.
Mog carried logs for the fire.
"We'll catch the mammoth now!" they yelled.
"We'll have our bite of pie!"

The mammoth thought, "I'd like to see them try!
There are six of them, six hungry men.
But they'll eat weeds and seeds again!
They have a spear to hit me.

They have a trap to trip me.
They have a cart to carry me.
They have a pot to hold me and a fire to bake me.
But they *still* can't catch me and put me in a pie.

Shall I tell you why?"
STOMP! STOMP! STOMP!
Over the mountain came the mammoth's mother.
STOMP! STOMP! STOMP! STOMP!

Over the mountain came his father, his brother.
His aunties, his uncles, his cousins, his friends.
And another and another and another!
Up the mountain stood sixty scary mammoths…

Down the mountain ran six scaredy cavemen!
Og broke the spear, Gog tripped the trap,
Ug and Bog upset the cart,
Nog kicked over the cooking pot.

Mog's dropped logs put out the fire.
And I am told that this is why
They never got their Mammoth Pie.
And when they cried out "What's for tea?"
Og grunted, "Weeds and seeds for me!"